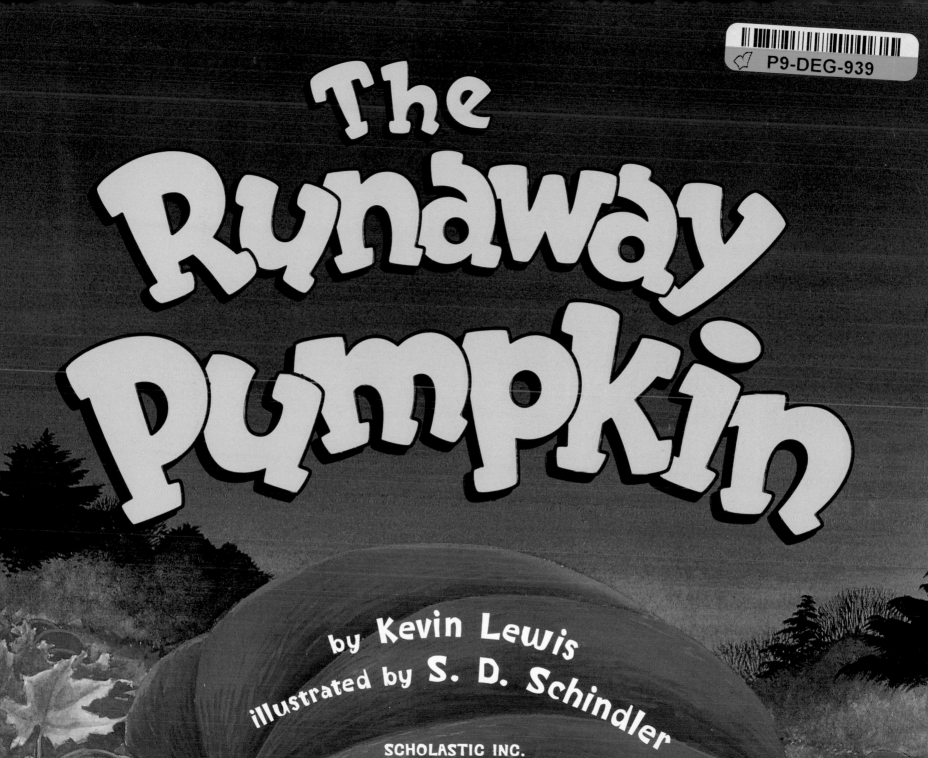

The Runaway Pumpkin

by Kevin Lewis

illustrated by S. D. Schindler

SCHOLASTIC INC.

New York · Toronto · London · Auckland · Sydney
Mexico City · New Delhi · Hong Kong · Buenos Aires

Once upon a hill,
when the wind blew with a chill

wandered Buck and Billy Baxter
with their baby sister, Lil.

And there, upon that hillside,
growing orange, fat, and fine
the budding Baxters found a pumpkin
on a twisty, twirly vine.

It was big and it was round,
and the boys, their eyes a-gleam,
gave a whoop, a yell, a holler
no finer pumpkin had they seen.

And today was Halloween.

Yet little Lil was cautious,
  and, of course, she tried to warn them,
    but her bumbling, big-head brothers
      snapped the pumpkin from its stem.

      And as she watched them roll it,
        at first real slow, but then much faster,
          little Lil looked down the hill
            and she foresaw disaster!

'Round and 'round
across the ground
makin' a
thumpin'
bumpin' sound
came that
thumpety
bumpety
thumpin'
bumpin'
round and roll-y
RUNAWAY PUMPKIN!

A short way down the hillside,
that zooming pumpkin caught the eye
of mucking Momma Baxter,
who thought of Granny's pumpkin pie

'til it BUSTED through her sty!

'Round and 'round
across the ground
makin' a
thumpin'
bumpin' sound
came that
thumpety,
bumpety
thumpin'
bumpin'
round and roll-y
RUNAWAY PUMPKIN!

A bit farther down the hillside,
just beyond the chicken coop,
Grampa Baxter saw that pumpkin
and thought of Granny's pumpkin soup

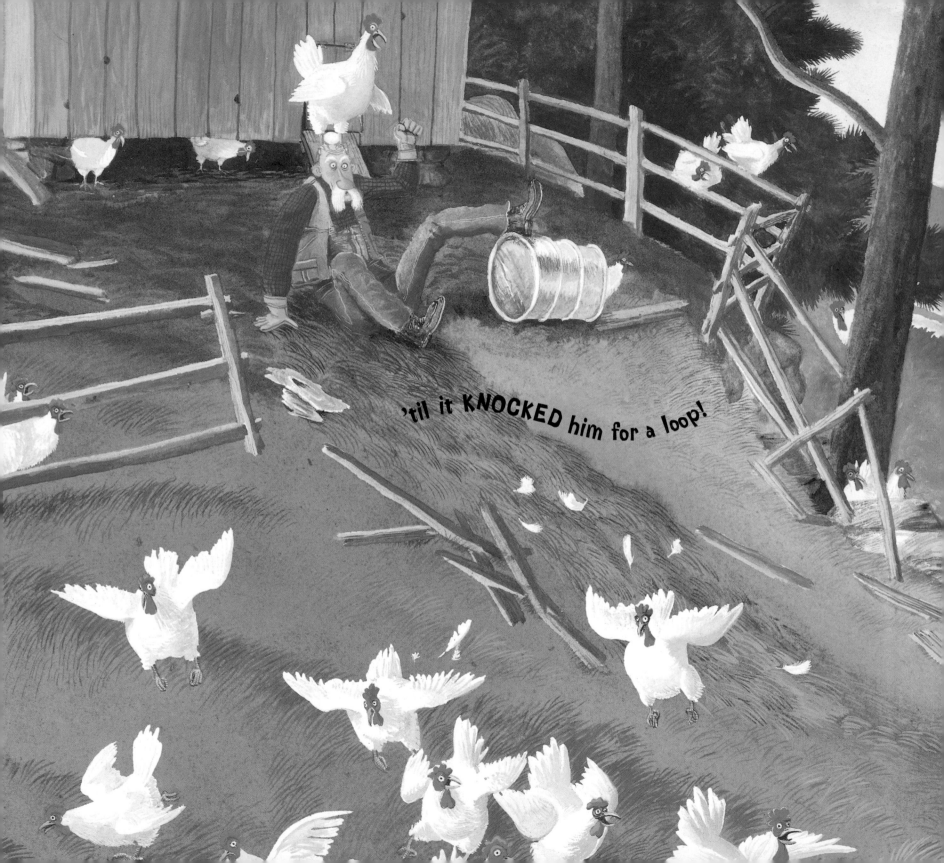

'til it KNOCKED him for a loop!

'Round and 'round
across the ground
makin' a
thumpin'
bumpin' sound
came that
thumpety

bumpety

thumpin'

bumpin'

round and roll-y

RUNAWAY PUMPKIN!

Now, at the bottom of that hillside,
where that boundin' pumpkin sped,
Poppa Baxter on his tractor
thought of Granny's pumpkin bread

but Poppa Baxter used his head
and quickly plowed a pumpkin bed!

So at the bottom of the hillside,
fat and round upon the ground,
that thumpin', bumpin' pumpkin plopped
and didn't make another sound.

And as pigs and hens and Baxters
gathered 'round where Poppa plowed
little Lil, she gathered Granny
and pulled her through the waiting crowd.

Buck and Billy looked really proud.

Then thumpety
bumpety
thumpin'
bumpin'
straight to the kitchen
went that pumpkin.

And soon after came the smell
of dear old Granny cookin' somethin'.

Granny stirred and stewed and baked
until the bright full moon rose up
and all those hungry Baxters
sat themselves right down to sup.

And at the center of the table,
among the soup and bread and pie,

Sat a grinning jack-o'-lantern with a twinkle in its eye.

For Ilana, Bella, Emma, Hannah, Grace, and all girls who are on a roll! — K. L.

557 Broadway, New York, NY 10012. ISBN 0-439-56544-8
Text copyright © 2003 by Kevin Lewis. Illustrations copyright © 2003 by S. D. Schindler. All rights reserved. Published by Scholastic Inc. SCHOLASTIC and associated logos are trademarks and/or registered trademarks of Scholastic Inc. • 12 11 10 9 8 7 6 5 4 3 2 1   3 4 5 6 7 8/0 • Printed in the U.S.A. 08 First Scholastic paperback printing, September 2003 • Book design by David Caplan The text type was set in SpleenyDecafGD. The title type was hand lettered by David Coulson.